A TO Z Animal Mysteries™

BATS IN THE CASTLE

SOLVE ANIMAL MYSTERIES
FROM A TO Z!

The Absent Alpacas
Bats in the Castle

RON ROY'S

A TO Z Animal MYSTERIES™

BATS IN THE CASTLE

WRITTEN BY
KAYLA WHALEY

ILLUSTRATED BY
CHLOE BURGETT

A STEPPING STONE BOOK™
Random House 🏠 New York

Text copyright © 2023 by Kayla Whaley
Cover art and interior illustrations copyright © 2023 by Chloe Burgett
Original A to Z Mysteries® series created by Ron Roy

Visit us on the Web!
rhcbooks.com

Educators and librarians, for a variety of teaching tools, visit us at
RHTeachersLibrarians.com

Library of Congress Cataloging-in-Publication Data
Names: Whaley, Kayla, author. | Roy, Ron. | Burgett, Chloe, illustrator.
Title: Bats in the castle / written by Kayla Whaley; illustrated by Chloe Burgett.
Description: New York: Random House, [2023] |
Series: Ron Roy's A to Z animal mysteries series | "A Stepping Stone book." |
Summary: "A high-pitched loud sound in an elevator shaft sends young sleuths Abbi, Daniel, and Lydia on the hunt for the source." —Provided by publisher.
Identifiers: LCCN 2022039985 (print) | LCCN 2022039986 (ebook) |
ISBN 978-0-593-48902-4 (trade) | ISBN 978-0-593-48903-1 (lib. bdg.) |
ISBN 978-0-593-48904-8 (ebook)
Subjects: CYAC: Bats—Fiction. | Mystery and detective stories. |
LCGFT: Detective and mystery fiction.
Classification: LCC PZ7.1.W4378 Bat 2023 (print) | LCC PZ7.1.W4378 (ebook) |
DDC [Fic]—dc23

MANUFACTURED IN CHINA
10 9 8 7 6 5 4 3 2

This book has been officially leveled by using the F&P Text Level Gradient™ Leveling System.

For Katie (and Connor!)
—K.W.

For James and Melissa
—C.B.

CHAPTER 1

Abigail "Abbi" Wallace held the walkie-talkie to her face. "Check, check. Come in, Lydia. Do you read me?"

The walkie-talkie buzzed to life. "Loud and clear, Captain. Copy," Lydia said. "We're all set up here. Over."

Abbi was sitting on the front porch of Moose Manor—the old castle where she lived with her mom, mystery writer Wallis Wallace, and their dog, Barkley. The sun was setting, and the air was chilly. Not bad for early October in Maine.

1

Normally, Abbi and her two best friends, Lydia and Daniel Herrera, would be up on the third-floor balcony. They all liked to watch the local bats come out for their nightly flight. Both the view and the sound quality were much better from up there.

But tonight, the elevator Abbi used to go upstairs was broken! It was old, just like the rest of the castle, and it didn't always work right. *Temperamental,* Abbi's mom liked to call it.

The repair people were coming to fix it soon. In the meantime, Abbi was stuck on the first floor. Again. A few years ago, she would have been able to walk up the stairs with some help. But the disease she was born with, called spinal muscular atrophy, caused her muscles to weaken over time, and now she always used her power wheelchair. So the elevator was the only way she could go upstairs.

"Okay, you opened the app on my phone? And plugged the mic in?" Abbi said into the walkie-talkie. "Nothing's red or blinking? There shouldn't be any blinking!"

"Looks good to me," Lydia said. "Hey, don't grab th—"

Daniel's voice came through. "Do you want us to take a picture so you can check we did it right?"

Abbi smiled. "That's okay. I trust you both!"

"Roger that. Be down soon," Daniel said.

Since Abbi couldn't be there herself, her friends were checking to make sure her recording equipment was ready for the night's action.

She had been recording animal sounds for as long as she could remember. First on a tape recorder. Later on her cell phone. But humans can't hear most bat sounds on their own. So for her birthday

a few months ago, her mom had bought her a special bat detection microphone to record the sounds bats made and transform them into something audible. It could even track the bats' flight paths based on their calls!

This was the first weekend she wouldn't be on the balcony to record things herself. But her friends were here for a sleepover, and at least her collection would still be complete.

Abbi turned off the walkie-talkie and set it on a little table next to her mug of hot cocoa.

"Boo!" Lydia said from behind her.

Abbi didn't flinch.

"Aw, I can never scare you!" Lydia
whined.

"That's because I can always hear
you coming," Abbi said, laughing.

Lydia and Daniel took their seats on
the porch's swinging bench.

"We didn't miss it, did we?" Lydia

asked. She scanned the darkening sky, looking for bats.

Daniel nudged her shoulder. "The sun's not even all the way down yet!"

"Maybe they're early risers—you don't know!"

Abbi shook her head. "Not this bunch. I've never seen them come out before sundown."

As if on cue, as the sun fully dipped below the horizon, a black cloud rose in the distance.

"Look!" Lydia said, pointing excitedly.

Abbi leaned forward in her wheelchair and smiled. "Showtime."

CHAPTER 2

After the bats had flown off for their nightly hunt, the kids went back inside. Lydia ran upstairs to get Abbi's phone and mic, while Daniel and Abbi decided on snacks for the rest of the evening.

"Chips?" Daniel asked, looking into the pantry. Barkley sat dutifully at his feet, hoping for a treat.

"We had chips with lunch," Abbi said. "Popcorn?"

Daniel shook his head. "It gets stuck in Lydia's teeth. We'd have to listen to her complain about it all night."

Abbi laughed. "Good point."

Wallis Wallace, Abbi's mom, strolled into the kitchen. She was balancing her laptop on one arm and holding a mug in the other hand. A familiar sight when she was on a book deadline!

"What would bats snack on?" Wallis asked as she headed for the stove.

"Fruit! That's a great idea, Mom!" Abbi said, then paused. "Or insects."

"Mmm, delicious," Abbi's mom said, smiling.

Lydia bounded back into the kitchen

and placed Abbi's phone in front of her on the table. "What's delicious?"

"Bugs," Daniel said.

"Hey, bugs *can* be delicious, you know!" Lydia replied.

Wallis moved the teakettle from the counter onto a burner. "That's true! But sadly, we don't have any fried silkworms or caterpillars on hand."

Daniel grabbed two pears and a red apple from the fruit bowl on the counter and stood between his sister and Abbi. "Fruit it is, then."

Barkley settled under the table. Maybe someone would slip him a bite of apple peel or a chunk of juicy pear!

Abbi opened the recording app on her phone and clicked on

the most recent file. Two graphs popped
up on the screen.

"What does all that mean?" Lydia
asked, pointing at the images.

Daniel leaned over for a better view.
"This wave on the top looks like what we
learned about in science," he said. "See
how it goes up and down?"

"Exactly!" Abbi said. "These are the sound waves the bats make. And then this other one shows the frequency—or at what pitch the sounds are. Bat calls are *really* high-pitched."

"What's that second graph called again, Abs?" Wallis said from the stove, waiting for her water to boil.

"A spectrogram!"

"Such a good word," Wallis said, mostly to herself. "I need to write that one down so I don't forget it again." She wandered into the living room.

Abbi used the touchscreen to scroll through different images. She frowned. "Something doesn't look right, though."

"What's wrong?" Lydia asked.

"The waves." Abbi pointed to the top graph. "They're too long to be from a bat, and the amplitude seems too high."

Lydia tilted her head. *"Amplitude* sounds familiar. Did we learn about that, too?"

Abbi nodded. "It means the height of the wave. Oh, I hope nothing got messed up! Maybe I didn't set the right threshold?"

Daniel looked at his sister and raised a brow. Lydia shrugged. She didn't understand any of this, either.

"Let's listen to it," Daniel said.

Abbi nodded. Her finger hovered over the play button.

Just then, an ear-piercing whistle filled the kitchen! All three of them jumped.

"Oh no, the recording *is* messed up!" Lydia said.

"I haven't even pressed *play* yet!" Abbi said.

Wallis ran back into the room.

She launched herself toward the stove and grabbed the hissing teakettle off the burner.

"Sorry!" she said. "The water's finally ready."

Abbi, Lydia, and Daniel each let out a breath, then giggled at their reactions. The sound was only the kettle, after all.

Abbi tapped the play button. But the sound was even worse than the hissing teakettle had been!

The twins covered their ears. Wallis nearly dropped her mug. Barkley whined from under the table before scurrying into the living room.

"Turn it off!" Lydia shouted.

Abbi smashed the stop button. The horrible screech echoed from the kitchen tiles, finally drifting back into silence.

"What *was* that?" Daniel asked. "That didn't sound like a bat to me."

"I don't know," Abbi said. "But the GPS tracker says it was coming from inside the house!"

CHAPTER 3

"What?!" Daniel and Lydia shouted at the same time. Their voices always sounded most alike when they were startled.

Wallis walked over to the table. She squatted next to Abbi to see the screen. "Inside where?" Wallis asked.

Abbi zoomed in on the map. "I can't tell for sure, but see this blue dot? That's where the sound came from." The dot was inside a square on the map.

17

She pointed at the shape. "And this is the castle. So the sound definitely came from somewhere in or near the house!"

Wallis stood and took a sip of her fresh tea. "Emory Scott strikes again," she said in a dramatic voice.

"Who?" Daniel asked.

Abbi rolled her eyes and returned her attention to the app. "He's the one who built this place. Mom thinks his ghost still lives here."

Lydia squeaked, "That sound was a *ghost*?"

Wallis laughed and gave Lydia a gentle pat on the shoulder. "More likely there was just something wrong with Abbi's recording app."

Abbi frowned. "There's nothing wrong with my app!"

Wallis shrugged. "Then it was a plane. Or maybe . . ." She headed toward the living room, where Barkley was still hiding from the scary noise. "Maybe Emory just wanted to say hi."

She grinned and went back to her office. The three kids were left in the kitchen with Wallis's words and the memory of the haunting noise echoing around them.

—

After finishing their fruit, they settled in Abbi's room. It was originally a guest room, so it was smaller than the other bedrooms. But it was the only one on the first floor! And since the elevator broke so often, it was easier for her to sleep down here.

She liked her room. It was cozy. The blue walls were covered with posters and framed drawings of animals. Leafy plants

dotted the shelves around the room. And strings of twinkling fairy lights hung above her bed!

But sometimes she wished she could be on one of the upper floors like her mom. She wanted to have a nice view of the forest on one side or the ocean on the other. Down here, all she could see out her window was the driveway.

"Do you really think that sound we heard was just a plane?" Lydia asked.

Daniel sat down next to his sister on Abbi's bed. "You're still thinking about that?" he asked.

"You *aren't?*" Lydia shuddered. "I'll probably have nightmares about that sound!"

Abbi looked at her phone. She'd been thinking about the mysterious sound, too.

"I guess it could have been a plane," she said uncertainly. "But an airplane would have created nonstop sound over a much longer period of time."

Lydia hopped off the bed. "Then it *is* a ghost!"

Barkley startled at the outburst. He was curled up on his doggie bed next to Abbi's desk.

Daniel laughed. "The only options are plane or ghost?"

"Or my app is broken," Abbi said, remembering what her mom had said in the kitchen. "But I just tested it yesterday!"

Lydia began pacing the small room.

Her ponytail went *swish* every time she spun back in the opposite direction.

"I don't think I'll be able to sleep tonight," she said. "I really don't."

Daniel flopped down onto the mattress. He flung his arms wide and sighed. "That means nobody will sleep."

Lydia shot a glare his way but kept pacing.

Abbi looked from one friend to the other. Barkley snored in the corner.

"Will you feel better if we prove the noise wasn't a ghost?" Abbi asked.

Lydia stopped walking and nodded hard.

"Then I guess this sleepover just became Operation Ghostbusters," Abbi said.

CHAPTER 4

"Is it working?" Lydia's voice asked through the tablet. "Can you see?"

"Try not to move so much!" Abbi said. "The video's all wobbly."

Abbi's tablet was open in front of her on the kitchen table. Barkley was playing with a stuffed toy at her feet.

Meanwhile, Lydia and Daniel were upstairs again with Abbi's phone and mic. Their own phones were duct-taped to the hard hats they were wearing, which they'd found in the mudroom. Through

the twins' phone cameras, she could see
everything they were seeing!

She couldn't be with them, and a
video call was the next-best option. But
whenever they moved too much, the
video got all blurry. It was hard to make
out details.

"Can you lean closer, Lydia? Just a
bit?"

The video feed on the left of Abbi's
screen zoomed in.

"No, no! That's too much! I just need to see the app better."

The plan was supposed to be simple: Lydia and Daniel would start recording in the same spot as before, but this time they would stay with the equipment. Abbi was hoping she'd be able to see or hear something useful. But it was hard to make sure the settings were right from here!

"*Ugh,*" Abbi said. "If I could just be up there with you, this would be easy!"

Daniel swung around, and his face appeared in his video feed. He looked worried. "Want us to come back down? We can just play a game or something instead."

Abbi chewed on her lip. She

didn't want to be the reason they stopped searching.

Just then, the strange noise blared through the screen!

Barkley and Lydia yelped at the same time.

"Sorry!" Lydia said. "I don't know what I pressed! Let me try to turn it off."

"Wait! This is good," Abbi said. "We can follow the sound."

Daniel turned the volume down so it wasn't blaring anymore. "Follow it how?" he asked.

Abbi explained that if he and Lydia walked around with the phone, they could see whether the sound got louder or quieter by looking at the waves in the graph. The higher the wave, the closer they were to the source.

"It's like playing hot or cold," Daniel said.

Abbi snapped her fingers. "Exactly. Now, follow that noise!"

—

The good news was that the sound was definitely coming from inside the house. The bad news? Lydia refused to go anywhere near it.

"I didn't sign up for *chasing* a ghost!"

Daniel sighed. "If we're gonna prove there isn't a ghost, we have to find out what *is* making the noise."

"Okay, so you can go by yourself." She shoved Abbi's phone and mic into Daniel's hands.

He shoved them right back.

"No!" Daniel said. "We can't split up! That's rule number one of scary movies."

"So you *are* scared!" Lydia cried.

"Hey, listen!" Abbi shouted at her screen. They turned their attention to

her. "What if I send Barkley up with you?
He can protect you."

Barkley ran over to Abbi at the sound
of his name. He barked once.

"Hear that? He said
he'd be happy to help!"
Abbi said, patting his
head.

While Lydia thought
about it, the mysterious
noise droned on in the
background. It would
stop sometimes, then start up moments
later. The rhythm of it was strangely
familiar.

Lydia sighed loud and long. "Fiiiiine.
Tell Barkley to come find us." She leaned

toward her brother's face, staring straight at Abbi through the phone camera on his hard hat. "But if a ghost gets me, I'm blaming you, Abbi!"

Abbi nodded. "That sounds fair to me. Get up there, Barkley! Keep them safe, boy!"

CHAPTER 5

Lydia, Daniel, and Barkley had been wandering the upper floors for the past hour and weren't any closer to finding the source. Back in the kitchen, Abbi was starting to get a little motion sick from watching through her friends' cameras the whole time.

"Don't you think the sound was louder near Wallis's room?" Daniel asked.

"No, it was for sure louder near our rooms!" Lydia said.

The twins visited so often that they

had their own bedrooms. Most of the time, they just slept on the floor of Abbi's room, but Wallis always said there was no reason to have such a big house if no one was using it!

"But we were just down our hallway!" Daniel said.

Abbi rested her head on her fist. She was getting frustrated again. Even if she could see the waves on the graph, there would be no way to pinpoint the location from down here in the kitchen. If only she could be up there with them!

"Dang elevator," she mumbled.

Wallis walked in for another refill. "What was that, honey?"

"Oh, nothing, Mom!" Abbi sighed. She didn't want her mom to feel bad about the elevator not working. It wasn't *her* fault the thing was ancient!

On the tablet, Daniel and Lydia were still debating which way to go next. Wallis leaned over and waved at them through

the screen. "How's the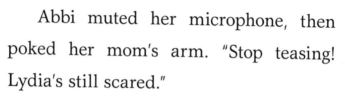
search going? Find Emory's
ghost yet?"

Abbi muted her microphone, then poked her mom's arm. "Stop teasing! Lydia's still scared."

"Who's teasing? I've been wanting to find a ghost here ever since I moved in!" she said. "What's the point of living in an old castle if it's not haunted, right?"

Wallis ruffled her daughter's hair before grabbing a cookie from the counter and heading back to her office.

"Hey! Hey, Abbi!" Daniel said. "I think we've got something!"

She unmuted her tablet and sat forward. "What did you find?"

The twins started running. The hallway's wood paneling and floral wallpaper blurred around them. Abbi felt queasy again, but she didn't want to look away and miss seeing whatever they were chasing.

"Technically *we* didn't find anything," Lydia clarified. "Barkley did! He just took off all of a sudden!"

That *was* strange! Barkley  liked chewing and getting his belly scratched way more than running.

"Barkley, wait up!" Lydia called.

They both slammed to a stop once they reached Barkley. Abbi tried to get her bearings through the screen. Both Lydia and Daniel were leaning over, trying to catch their breath, so their cameras were pointed at the ground.

"What is it?" she asked, unable to wait. "What did he find?"

Daniel stood up first. Abbi focused on his side of the screen.

"Nothing," he said. "He just led us to the end of the hall. See? We're just at the elevator."

Abbi's shoulders drooped. "A dead end."

She could see through Lydia's camera that Barkley was still on alert, though! His tail was wagging, and his ears were pricked up. He looked ready to play. But why would he have run here for that?

"Abbi, isn't this elevator, like, *super* old?" Lydia asked.

"Yeah, Mom says it was one of the first elevators built in Maine."

Lydia smacked her brother's arm. "I *told you* it was a ghost!"

"Ow!" Daniel said. "And how does an old elevator equal ghost, Lyddie Bug?"

Lydia slowly backed away from the elevator door. "If you were a ghost, wouldn't you hide in a creepy old elevator shaft? I would."

"I truly don't understand how your brain works sometimes," he said. "Why would a ghost stay in an elevator shaft when there's an entire castle to haunt?"

"I dunno." Lydia threw her hands up. "Maybe the elevator is cozy! It's dark and creepy, right? Perfect haunting conditions."

"*Why* would a *ghost* need somewhere cozy? They're a ghost!"

Abbi let their bickering fade into the background. She felt an idea tugging at the back of her mind.

"Somewhere dark and creepy," she repeated to herself. "Dark and creepy and . . ."

Her head snapped up.

"That's it!" Abbi shouted. "I think I know what the noise is."

CHAPTER 6

The next morning, Abbi and her friends were gathered around the elevator on the first floor. Some mechanics had arrived to repair it! But more importantly, Park Ranger Woo had arrived, too.

"You're sure there's a bat in here? How did you figure it out?" she asked Wallis.

"Oh, I didn't," Wallis answered. She took a bite of the buttered croissant she was holding. "My brilliant daughter did."

Abbi smiled softly and blushed. "It was pretty obvious once Barkley led us to the elevator. A bat call would bounce all over the walls in an elevator shaft. Of course it would sound weird on the app! I should've realized sooner."

Daniel knelt down next to Barkley and petted his head. The dog snuggled into him. "Abbi and Barkley are quite a team."

"We're all a team!" Abbi protested.

Lydia nodded. "What will happen to the bat?" she asked.

"If there really is a bat in there—" Park Ranger Woo said.

"There is," Abbi said.

The woman continued, "We'll find it a new home."

One of the elevator mechanics

dropped a tool, and everyone jumped at the loud *clank* on the floor. The sound bounced way up to the rafters. Abbi hoped it didn't scare the bat inside.

Daniel wandered closer to watch how the elevator mechanics would get the door open without power.

"There are bats that live near the lake," Abbi said. "Can you release it there?"

The ranger folded her arms and leaned against the wall. "That's probably where the bat came from, which means its habitat likely isn't safe anymore."

Lydia said, "What? Why not?"

Park Ranger Woo sighed—a long, sad sound. "There's a fungal disease called white-nose syndrome, which bats can get. It's been infecting a lot of colonies around here. Once it spreads in an area, sometimes the healthy bats will leave the group and try to find shelter on their own. Like in an attic or—"

"Or an elevator shaft," Abbi said.

The woman nodded.

Wallis put her hand to her chest. "Oh, that's awful. The poor thing. All alone, nowhere safe to go. Separated from all its friends."

Abbi thought about the night before. She'd been all alone, too. Separated from her friends while they went on this big adventure. And in her own home! Even when the elevator *was* working, it was kind of scary to use.

"I think I know how the bat feels," she said. She hadn't meant to say it out loud! But Wallis and Lydia both heard her.

"What do you mean, sweetheart?" Wallis asked.

Abbi could have lied. She could have said she was joking or made up some other answer. But instead, she took a deep breath and said, "Sometimes I wish I didn't have to worry about the elevator breaking so much. It would be nice if I didn't have to be stuck on the first floor."

Lydia put a gentle hand on Abbi's shoulder.

Wallis looked shocked for a moment. But then she said, "You're absolutely right. We should have replaced this old thing ages ago. I'm sorry I didn't think of it myself. Once we get this bat moved somewhere safe, we'll work on finding a new elevator! State-of-the-art!"

Abbi sat up straight. "Really, Mom?" She couldn't believe it!

Wallis nodded. "Matter of fact, I'll start researching right now. You can handle this bat issue, right, Abbi?"

"Of course!"

The park ranger looked from mother to daughter and shrugged. "As long as I can capture whatever's in there safely, I don't mind who's here to watch."

"Hey, look over here!" Daniel said. "They're ready to open the elevator!"

Everyone watched eagerly as the doors slowly opened.

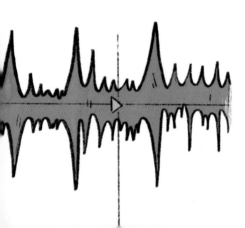

CHAPTER 7

Once the elevator doors were open, Park Ranger Woo went to work. She asked everyone to stay back until she'd caught whatever animal was in there.

"It's a bat," Abbi muttered again.

"All the more reason to clear the area, then," Park Ranger Woo said kindly. "Bats can have rabies or parasites. You wouldn't want to get exposed to any of that!"

Abbi nodded and drove toward the other end of the hall. Daniel followed.

Barkley tried to sneak a little closer to the action, but Lydia gently snagged his collar, holding him back. "We gotta let her work, boy. Abbi, should I take Barkley outside? He might spook the bat."

"Good call," Abbi said. "I'll be out there soon. I wanna see what Park Ranger Woo does!"

The woman walked back to the three friends. She had put on heavy-duty work gloves and was carrying a small plastic container—the kind you might pack a sandwich in for lunch!—with tiny holes poked into the lid.

"There's not gonna be much to see yet," she said. "I think your bat is roosting toward the top of the shaft, so I'm heading upstairs."

Abbi deflated. Once again, she was going to miss out on all the action!

Park Ranger Woo saw the disappointment on Abbi's face and said brightly, "How about you all wait outside, and I'll come find you once I'm done."

"Okay," Abbi said, pouting more than she would like.

Daniel gave a thumbs-up to Park Ranger Woo. "Good luck!"

—

An hour later, the kids were sipping freshly brewed apple cider on the front

porch, overlooking the moat. Barkley, happily chowing down on his own dried apple chips, snapped his head up and thumped his tail excitedly.

Abbi glanced toward the door and saw Park Ranger Woo coming out. She was carrying the plastic container, and there was something in it!

"Look! She did it!" Abbi cried.

"Of course I did," Park Ranger Woo said. "Where's your mom? I assume you all want to take a look at our little friend."

Lydia chugged the last of her cider and came to kneel close to Abbi. She was still scared of whatever was haunting the house!

Wallis's voice rang out from somewhere above them. The balcony off her office, Abbi guessed. "I'll be right down!"

As they waited for Abbi's mom, Park Ranger Woo carefully set the container

on the table. The plastic was cloudy. It was hard to make out what was inside except for a small, dark shape.

"Was it a bat?" Abbi asked. "It was a bat, right?"

The woman laughed. "It was a bat."

Abbi fist pumped, and Lydia let out a long, relieved sigh.

Daniel leaned over the table, close to the lid. "How did you get it out?" He reached toward the container before quickly thinking better of it and pulling his hand back.

"The poor little thing must be exhausted," Park Ranger Woo said. "It was sound asleep, but I think less from sleepiness and more from stress."

"But it's day-time," Abbi said. "Bats are nocturnal. They sleep during the day and fly around at night."

Park Ranger Woo nodded. "True, but even when I went to trap her, she didn't wake up or try to get away, as most bats would do. She had too little energy."

Lydia slid to the other side of the table and crouched down so her eyes were at table level. "Is it sick?"

"I don't know. Probably just hungry and scared, but the vet will find out for sure."

The front door opened again, and they heard Wallis's quick steps heading toward them. "Speaking of hungry, I

brought some fruit for our guest! I heard
bats like fruit."

Park Ranger Woo started to speak,
but Abbi interrupted. "Mom, only *some*
bats like fruit! It depends on what kind
of bat they are!"

The park ranger smiled and took a green pear from the basket Wallis was carrying. She chomped into it herself. "Right again. And this is a little brown bat, which means—"

"It only eats insects!" Abbi said.

Abbi felt a blush of pride when Park Ranger Woo nodded. But then Abbi's smile faded. "Oh, it must have been *starving*," she cried. "Little brown bats usually eat a ton! They have to eat half their weight in bugs every night. There's no way that many bugs would be living in the elevator shaft!"

Lydia shuddered. "Yikes! I hope not."

"Exactly," Park Ranger Woo said to Abbi. "So let's take a peek real quick, and then I'll get her to the vet."

The woman
still had her big
work gloves on. "I'm
going to very gently lift the lid.
Try not to make any sudden noises or
movements. I don't want to wake the
poor thing and risk her flying away before we can get her checked out."

"Her?" Daniel asked.

"Her. You can tell because the females
are bigger than the males." Park Ranger

Woo slowly popped the lid and peeled it
back. "See?"

Inside the container slept a tiny crea-
ture covered with glossy reddish-brown
fur. She was smaller than Abbi expected.

She probably wouldn't fit in Abbi's hand,
but Uncle Walker could hold her easily in
one palm. Her face was a little smooshed,
almost like a pug's. Hairless black wings
were tucked under her as she dozed.

Lydia clapped her hands
to her mouth to muffle
her squealing. She
whispered, "She's so
cute!"

Abbi wanted to
touch her fur to see
if it was as soft as it
looked, but she knew
that would be dangerous
for her *and* the bat.

"Will you be able to release her again

after she gets better?" Abbi asked, making sure to keep her voice low.

Abbi, Daniel, Lydia, and Wallis all looked expectantly at Park Ranger Woo. Only Barkley had returned to what he'd been doing before, chewing on his treats.

"Hopefully. We'll have to decide the best place. And in the meantime, I'm gonna do a check on some of the nearby caves. See if there are any fungus out-breaks we should know about."

Abbi looked down at the sleeping bat. She seemed so out of place

in the little plastic tub. Not at all where she belonged.

"Sleep well, little bat," Abbi said softly. "I hope I get to hear what you sound like when you're free someday."

CHAPTER 8

A week later, Abbi, Lydia, and Daniel were on the front lawn of the castle, near the moat bridge. Barkley was napping in the last patch of late-afternoon sunlight on the grass.

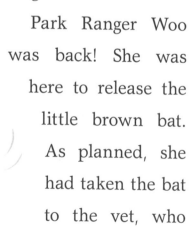

Park Ranger Woo was back! She was here to release the little brown bat. As planned, she had taken the bat to the vet, who suggested plenty of rest and a steady diet of insect goodness. And now the bat had a clean bill of health and was ready to move into her new home!

"Do you think she'll like it?" Lydia asked, looking up at the castle walls.

Abbi nodded. "Definitely! Bat houses are specifically made for bats!"

The bat house was simple. It was a plain wooden box about two feet high and four feet wide. It was painted black to absorb the heat from the sun and keep a bat warm, especially during its winter hibernation.

Abbi and Wallis had debated a lot over *where* to place the new bat house. With some advice from Park Ranger Woo, they had finally decided to install it under the eaves on the third floor.

Daniel pointed to the window closest to where Park Ranger Woo was carefully balancing on a tall, sturdy ladder outside the castle. "Isn't that gonna be your new room, Abbi?"

Abbi grinned. "Yep! As soon as the new elevator gets up and running."

Once Wallis had learned how unhappy Abbi was about being stuck on the first floor, she had sprung into action. She had called someone about upgrading their elevator the very next day! It would take a while before it was finished, but

Abbi didn't mind waiting. Soon she'd have the same view as their new bat neighbor: overlooking the castle's moat and the dense forest, all the way to the horizon.

Lydia plopped down on the ground. They'd been out here for a while. Her legs must have gotten tired. Not everyone got to bring a comfy chair with them everywhere, as Abbi did!

"Do you think more bats will join ours?" Lydia asked.

Daniel sat on Abbi's other side. "Can we really call her *ours*? She's not a pet."

Abbi's actual pet, Barkley, glanced at them sleepily. Then Abbi watched him drift back to sleep. "You're right," she said. "She's not a pet. Ours or anyone else's."

Lydia made a humming noise, as if she was thinking. "Can't we give her a name, though? Everyone deserves a name."

They all thought quietly for a moment. Park Ranger Woo seemed to be tightening the final screws. Behind them, the sun was sinking quickly, throwing long purple shadows over the lawn and onto the walls of the castle.

"What about Emory Scott?" Abbi asked. "Or just Emory for short."

"Like the ghost?" Lydia asked with a shiver.

Daniel reached up and gave Abbi a high five.

Just then, Park Ranger Woo called out to them, "Here we go! You all ready?"

They whooped in response and pulled out their phones. Lydia and Daniel were going to take pictures, but Abbi had her bat-recording app open.

Standing on the ladder, Park Ranger Woo pulled her work gloves from her pocket and slipped them on. Then, cradling the container in the crook of her arm, she said, "Three, two, one!"

As soon as she opened the lid, a refreshed and energized little brown bat zoomed out

and perched on the ledge of her new bat house. She paused for a moment, getting her bearings. Then she swooped down over their heads, off to her nightly hunt.

"Welcome home, Emory," Abbi said.

BAT FACTS FROM A TO Z!

- *Bananas, avocados, and mangoes, oh my!* Bats help pollinate more than three hundred species of fruit. They also spread seeds that help nuts grow.

- Did you know that bats are the only mammals that can fly? (The flying squirrel doesn't actually fly—it glides!)

- *Zoom, zoom!* Bats can fly almost one hundred miles per hour.

- A group of bats is called a *colony,* and their babies are called *pups.*

- Bats, like most mammals, have *belly buttons*!

- *Sleeping upside down* helps bats escape predators quickly.

- *Listen to see?* Bats use *echolocation* to "see" what's around them in the dark. They send out a sound and listen to the echo that comes back. To be able to fly at night, bats need both good eyesight and good hearing!

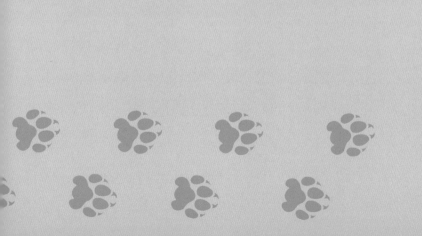

Follow the tracks to the next book!

A to Z Animal Mysteries™

COUGAR CLUES

"Welcome to Moose Manor!" Uncle Walker said as the TV crew got out of their van. His arms were flung wide in greeting.

Three people exited the vehicle.

Arthur Fitzpatrick shook Uncle Walker's hand. Then he smiled at Abbi and her two best friends. Daniel hid shyly behind his sister.

"It's a pleasure to meet you folks," the *Wild Whereabouts* host said. "Thanks for letting us visit your home."

"Oh, this isn't *our* home," Lydia said, pointing to herself and Daniel. "I'm just here in case you need any on-screen talent. And my brother's here because he's your biggest fan."

Daniel elbowed Lydia.

Arthur laughed. It was a warm, bright sound. "Is that so? It's an honor to meet you."

He introduced the two women who were with him. The sound engineer had long, curly dark hair and was named Amy. The camera operator, Steph, was the tallest person Abbi had ever seen! They both nodded politely, but they were mainly focused on unloading all their equipment.

And it was a lot of equipment! Big

cameras and handheld cameras. Tiny clip-on microphones and the large, fuzzy kind. Bags of doodads and whatsits. Plus three tents, neatly in their carrying cases, waiting to be set up in a clearing in the forest.

"All right, kids," Uncle Walker said, "let's help our new friends transport all this to their campsite."

"No, no!" Arthur said. He held up his hands to wave off the offer. "We can manage it."

Abbi, who had been too nervous even to say hello, scanned the various bags and boxes. "You could hang some of those duffels on the handles of my wheelchair," she said eagerly, pointing.

Daniel jumped out from behind

Lydia. "Yeah, Abbi's great at carrying things!" He reached for the nearest piece of luggage, a black duffel with a small sunflower stitched on the side. Before he could pick it up, Arthur grabbed the bag.

Arthur's face looked shocked and almost scared. Abbi knew that people were sometimes uncomfortable when she offered help, so she gave him her most reassuring smile. "I really don't mind!"

"That's a very kind offer, but how about you help us navigate these woods instead?" His hand was still wrapped tightly around the handle of the sunflower bag. "We need to get the lay of the land before tonight."

"What happens tonight?" Lydia asked.

Before Arthur could answer, Abbi

said, "Cougars are mostly nocturnal. They only come out at night."

This earned her an impressed smile from Arthur. "Right you are! Which is why the *real* work begins at sunset."

He smiled, as if about to share a secret. "Who wants to catch a cougar?"

HAVE YOU READ ALL THE BOOKS IN THE

A to Z Mysteries®

SERIES?

Help Dink, Josh, and Ruth Rose . . .

. . . solve
mysteries
from A to Z!

Discover some magic in these page-turning adventures!

For budding
ballerinas!

For the
unicorn-obsessed!

For dog lovers
and budding pirates!

For cat lovers and
wannabe mermaids!

Find these books and more at rhcbooks.com!